The Ultimate

Marvel

Trivia & Fact Book

Hundreds of amazing facts about the Marvel Cinematic Universe, and hundreds more trivia questions about its characters, worlds and films.

J.M. Castle

Table of Contents

101 Fascinating Facts

About the Marvel Universe, its characters and its creators

Have you ever wondered about the masterminds behind the superheroes we know and love? How certain comics were created, how specific events altered the course of the MCU and the reasons why the characters are the way they are? In the following pages, you'll find 101 of the most fascinating facts about the world of Marvel, spanning across its foundation in the early 1900's to its latest box office hit, and all the years in between, filled with hundreds of characters across thousands of comics and dozens of incredible films. How do the Transformers fit into the Marvel Universe? Who did Tom Cruise audition to play? Why was She-Hulk invented? What do the Pet Shop Boys have to do with anything!? Read on to find out. Prepare to have your mind blown, with 101 facts you did not know about the crazy universe of Marvel.

1. Black Panther, The Avengers and The Avengers: Infinity War are all in the top 10 highest-grossing films of all time.

2. Marvel has had several different characters called Captain Marvel because if they do not regularly release a book with that title, DC will claim the trademark for its character of the same name.

3. Prior to joining the Avengers, Dr. Strange assembled a team known as The Defenders, which consisted of The Hulk, Silver Surfer and Namor.

4. Kevin Feige has produced every MCU film to date. He is also the one who invented the term 'MCU' (Marvel Cinematic Universe).

5. In the original story, Bruce Banner transformed into The Hulk at sundown, not when angered.

6. In the movie Captain America: Winter Soldier, Steve Rogers is writing a list of cultural events to catch up on after being on ice for decades. Depending on which country you watch the movie, different cultural events will be shown on the list.

7. For example, on Captain America's list, 'Steve Jobs (Apple)' appears on the American version of the film, whilst 'Berlin Wall up-down' appears on the German iteration, and 'Steve Irwin' appears on the Australian version instead.

8. Since 2002, three different actors have played Spiderman across eight films. Tobey Maguire, Andrew Garfield and Tom Holland.

9. Wonder Woman, Captain America, Loki, Conan the Barbarian, Black Widow, Storm and Superman are all deemed worthy to wield Thor's Hammer.

10. For a brief time, Godzilla, the Transformers and Fu Manchu have all been included in the Marvel universe.

11. DC's Swamp-Thing and Marvel's Man-Thing debuted within days of each other. The creators of these characters were roommates at the time.

12. Mystique is a shapeshifter and is the mother of Nightcrawler, although writer Chris Claremont originally intended her to be his father.

13. Terence Howard played James Rhodes in Iron Man. He was paid almost double what Robert Downey Jr. was payed for the film. This huge paycheque was the reason Don Cheadle replaced Howard in subsequent Iron Man flicks.

14. Kelly Sue DeConnick is the author of the Captain Marvel comic books, and has a cameo in the film her comics were adapted into.

15. Yellowjacket's lasers in Ant-Man make the same noise as the AT-AT's in Star Wars.

16. X-Men may belong to Marvel, but Fox holds the rights to transform the comic books into a movie.

17. Luke Cage was released in 1972, and was the very first African-American superhero to feature his own comic.

18. At one point, Spiderman was going to be called Insect-Man or even Fly-Man.

19. Daredevil originally had a sidekick. A seeing-eye dog named Deuce the Devil Dog.

20. Stan Lee chose to put a hyphen in Spider-Man's name to make it look different to Superman.

21. In 1984, DC approached Marvel about potentially licensing the publishing rights to the entire DC Universe. DC came to the conclusion that Marvel were better suited to making successful comics of Batman and the Justice League, due to Marvel dominating the market at the time. However, Marvel declined due to the belief that the DC comics weren't selling very well due to the characters not being very good.

22. Martin Goodman, the founder of Marvel Comics, was meant to be aboard the Hindenburg the day it crashed, but changed his plans at the last second.

23. Martin Goodman did not like the concept of Spider-Man that Stan Lee pitched to him due to his belief that 'kids hate spiders'.

24. The villain Carnage is so powerful that Spiderman and Venom once had to make a truce to defeat him.

25. Black Bolt can run so fast that he becomes invisible to the naked eye. He's faster even than Quicksilver.

26. Mr. Fantastic and The Invisible Woman had a child called Franklin Richards.

27. Franklin Richards has the power to manipulate reality and is considered one of the most powerful beings in the entire universe.

28. Jean Grey has died 16 times throughout the Marvel Comics.

29. Game of Thrones author George R.R. Martin claimed he regularly wrote to Marvel's letter columns when he was growing up.

30. Stan Lee's full name was Stanley Martin Lieber, and he was born in New York City in 1922.

31. Endgame is the 7th film in the Marvel Cinematic Universe to hit the $1 billion mark worldwide.

32. Renowned actor Vin Diesel voices the character Groot throughout the Guardians of the Galaxy films.

33. Captain America has a round shield because his original shield was thought to be too similar to the costume of The Shield, a rival comics' superhero.

34. Joe Simon is the co-creator of Captain America. He claims the inspiration for Red Skull came from the cherry on top of a hot fudge sundae.

35. Both Marvel and DC share the trademark to the phrase 'Super-Hero'.

36. Longshot is his own grandfather. Shatterstar is also his own grandfather. They're both each other's father and son.

37. Disney purchased Marvel Entertainment in 2009 for $4 billion.

38. Marvel created Spider-Woman just to secure the trademark for her name.

39. The Marvel Cinematic Universe (MCU) is the highest-grossing film franchise of all time.

40. The Office star John Krasinski auditioned for the role of Captain America, before Marvel finally decided on Chris Evans.

41. The Avengers: Endgame holds the record for the highest opening weekend of any movie ever, earning an unprecedented 1.2 billion worldwide.

42. Chris Pratt lost 60 pounds (27 kilos) in 6 months to play the role of Peter Quill in the Guardians of the Galaxy film.

43. "I took the Chris Pratt approach to training for an action movie. Eliminate anything fun for a year and then you can play a hero." – Paul Rudd on preparing for the Ant-Man film.

44. Black Widow is also known as Natalia Romanova and Natasha Romanov.

45. Black Widow is close to 70 years old. She retains her youthful appearance thanks to a variation of the super-soldier serum.

46. Marvel used to publish a yearly swimsuit special featuring its superheroes.

47. When Punisher died, he was recruited by his families Guardian Angel to be heaven's assassin.

48. Loki was first introduced into the Marvel Universe 13 years prior to his brother Thor's first appearance.

49. The X-Men character Dazzler was created as a collaboration between Marvel Comics and Casablanca Studios. The idea was dropped when disco music popularity began to decline.

50. Marvel loopholed a law that increased taxes on toys that represented humans by claiming that X-Men figurines were in fact mutants, and not humans.

51. In the 70's, Filmnation had a cartoon in which they would create new superheroes to trademark potential names, as well as avoid licensing fees.

52. To protect his secret identity, Daredevil pretended to be his own (imaginary) twin brother, Mike Murdock.

53. X-Men No. 1 was published in 1991. It is the world's number one selling comic book. It has sold over 8 million copies.

54. The first film to be produced in the Marvel Cinematic Universe was Iron Man, in 2008, starring Robert Downey Jr.

55. The original Fantastic Four comprised of Spiderman, Ghost Rider, The Hulk and Wolverine.

56. In college, Peter Parker had the same IQ as Reed Richards when he was of the same age.

57. The Amazing Spider-Man 2 is the only Spiderman film that has been shot entirely in New York, which happens to be the characters home town.

58. Since the death of The Ancient One, Dr. Strange has become the Sorcerer Supreme and Guardian of the Universe.

59. The idea for Spider-Man's black costume was inspired by a fan of the comics in the 1980's. The black costume eventually evolved into Spider-Man's nemesis, Venom.

60. Larry Hama created the characters for G.I. Joe for Hasbro. Larry is also the writer of the licenced comics published by Marvel Comics. Larry's idea of G.I. Joe was originally meant to be a new direction for Nick Fury and S.H.I.E.L.D.

61. The backstory for Transformers and the majority of its characters were created by Marvel editors Jim Shooter, Danny O'Neil and Bob Budianksy.

62. According to Stan Lee, the main reason that Spiderman wears a mask is so that his enemies don't see when he's afraid.

63. T'Challa funds The Mutantes Sans Frontieres; an organisation that protects mutant rights. Which, in turn, funds the X-Men.

64. Prior to 2007, Marvel licenses out their Superheroes out to different studios, including Sony acquiring Spider-Man and 20th Century Fox borrowing the Fantastic Four, Elektra, Daredevil and X-Men.

65. Original Hulk actor Ed Norton refused offers to return to the MCU during Hulk crossovers, because he didn't want to get 'type-cast' in future roles.

66. Dunkirk, Harry Potter and Hamlet actor Kenneth Branagh directed Thor in 2011.

67. The events in The Incredible Hulk, Thor and Iron Man 2 all take place within the one week.

68. Liam Hemsworth auditioned for the role of Thor but was ultimately passed on for his brother Chris Hemsworth.

69. We first hear of the Avengers in the movie 'The Incredible Hulk'

70. The director of The Incredible Hulk originally wanted Mark Ruffalo as the star actor, but Marvel decided on Norton instead.

71. Benedict Cumberbatch plays both hero Dr. Strange AND the villain Dormammu in the film Doctor Strange.

72. It was Spiderman star Tom Holland's Instagram account that inspired the vlog-style intro to Spider-Man: Homecoming.

73. Neal Tennant is the lead singer of the musical group the 'Pet Shop Boys'. He was an editor at Marvel in the 70's.

74. Marvel Comics owned the rights to the word 'Zombie' from the 1970's through to the 1990's.

75. The Savage She-Hulk comic was invented purely to copyright the name.

76. The DC character Shazam was originally intended to be called Captain Marvel, but DC were unable to do this due to trademark disputes.

77. In 2007, Marvel planned 10 movies across the next 8 years, financing them in-house, and thus creating the new Marvel Cinematic Universe (MCU.)

78. From 2008-2018, Marvel has grossed over $17 million at the box office.

79. Marvel Comics was born in 1939, originally known as Timely Comics.

80. Michael Jackson tried to purchase Marvel Comics so that he could play Spider-Man in future films.

81. Black Panther is the highest-grossing film from a black director ever, and the 3rd highest-grossing of any film ever. Ryan Coogler has also directed Creed and is directing Space Jam 2, featuring LeBron James.

82. In the Marvel Comics, famous talk-show host Stephen Colbert once ran for president. In fact, he eventually won by popular vote.

83. Spider-Man actor Tom Holland has credited Mart McFly from the iconic Back to the Future franchise as his main inspiration for Peter Parker.

84. In Captain America: The Winter Soldier, the inscription on Nick Fury's tombstone 'Ezekiel 25:17' is a direct reference to Samuel L. Jackson's role in Pulp Fiction, in which he quotes the Bible passage.

85. Deadpool is not included in the MCU. He is not an Avenger. However, he is still trademarked by Marvel.

86. The X-Men franchise, whilst owned by Marvel, is not apart of the MCU.

87. Marvel has now branched out to the TV screen as well, including shows Marvel's Runaways, Marvel's Agents of S.H.I.E.L.D and Marvel's Daredevil.

88. Walt Disney Company have begun to include Marvel characters into their amusement parks.

89. Both Nicolas Cage and Tom Cruise were considered for the role of Iron Man, but Robert Downy Jr. ultimately received the role.

90. The Russo brothers directed The Winter Soldier, Civil War, Infinity War and Endgame. Prior to these Marvel movies, the brothers were involved with television projects such as Arrested Development and Community.

91. Howard Stern tried, and failed, to acquire the rights to Ant-Man.

92. The name of the cat in the Captain Marvel movie is named Goose, which is a reference to the co-pilot in the film 'Top-Gun' (1986).

93. Hulk was originally grey, but was later turned greened due to colour separation issues in the 1960's comics.

94. The Incredible Hulk (2008), starring actor Ed Norton, didn't dominate the box office as expected, and plans for subsequent films were cancelled.

95. Peyton Reed, director of films including Bring It On and The Break-Up, was chosen to direct Ant-Man. Shaun of the Dead director Edgar Wright was also considered for the task, but was unsuccessful.

96. The Sony computers were hacked in 2014, revealing key plot points in upcoming films, including plans to incorporate Spiderman into the MCU. Indeed, Spiderman was featured in Captain America: Civil War later that year.

97. In 1992, Wesley Snipes proclaimed intentions to make and star in a Black Panther film. After a decade of discussions, the idea was never resulted.

98. The Coal Tiger was the original name of the character Black Panther.

99. The Spider-Man film franchise is the 10th highest-grossing franchise of all time, grossing over $5 billion to date.

100. Thor was created by Stan Lee to create a character stronger than the Hulk. "The only way to make a character stronger than the strongest man in the world, is to make that character a God."

101. There are estimated to be over 32,000 comics published by Marvel Comics over a period of 70 years (1939-2009), although official figures are unknown.

101 Trivia Questions

About the Marvel Universe, its characters and its films

So, do you consider yourself a casual fan of the Marvel movies? Or do you see yourself as a Marvel elite, knowing every quote, every scene, and every detail of every character to ever grace the cinema screen within the Marvel universe. The following 101 questions will put your knowledge to the test. Whether you're new to Marvel, or a die-hard fan, there'll be questions that you'll know and that will stump you. What is Captain Marvel's real name? Who invented the Super-Soldier serum? Who voiced Rocket in the Guardians of the Galaxy films? These questions and many, many more await. Test yourself or your friends, and prove who the true master of Marvel is!

In which MCU film did Samuel L. Jackson first appear as Nick Fury?

A)   Iron Man

B)   Black Panther

C)   The Incredible Hulk

D)   Guardians of the Galaxy

In which city did Iron Man first fight Whiplash?

A)   Beijing

B)   Monaco

C)   Toronto

D)   Venice

What was the name of the crew of mercenaries that raised Star-Lord?

A)   The Raiders

B)   The Ravagers

C)   The Reavers

D)   The Riders

A) Iron Man   B) Monaco   B) The Ravagers

Which of the Infinity Stones is colored orange?

A)   Mind Stone

B)   Power Stone

C)   Reality Stone

D)   Soul Stone

Who played Nebula in the 'Guardians of the Galaxy' films?

A)   Karen Gillan

B)   Scarlet Johansson

C)   Summer Glau

D)   Zoe Saldana

Which MCU film is the shortest in the franchise at just 112 minutes long?

A)   Ant-Man And The Wasp

B)   Captain America: Civil War

C)   Doctor Strange

D)   Thor: The Dark World

D) Soul Stone   A) Karen Gillan   D) Thor: The Dark World

What is Thor's hammer called?

A)   Baldr

B)   Gungnir

C)   Mjolnir

D)   Skofnung

Who is Bruce Banner's love interest during The Incredible Hulk?

A)   Betty Ross

B)   Bobbi Morse

C)   Claire Temple

D)   Maria Hill

"Until such time as the world ends, we will act as though it intends to spin on." Who said this quote?

A)   Hank Pym

B)   Jasper Sitwell

C)   Nick Fury

D)   Tony Stark

"Some believe that before the universe, there was nothing. They're wrong. There was darkness… and it survived." Who said this quote?

A)   Loki

B)   Odin

C)   Nebula

D)   Thanos

Who is Quicksilvers' sister?

A)   Betty Ross

B)   Gamora

C)   Pepper Potts

D)   Scarlet Witch

Who winds up with the Aether by the end of 'Thor: The Dark World'?

A)   Hawkeye

B)   Jane Foster

C)   The Collector

D)   Thor

B) Odin   D) Scarlet Witch   C) The Collector

What is the name of the group of soldiers that Captain America led during World War II?

A)   The Dire Elite

B)   The Howling Commandos

C)   The Juggernauts

D)   The Mad Crusaders

What color is the Time Stone?

A)   Blue

B)   Green

C)   Red

D)   Yellow

In what year was Thor: Ragnarok released?

A)   2011

B)   2013

C)   2015

D)   2017

Ronan the Accuser is of what race?

A)   Chitauri

B)   Kree

C)   Sakaarans

D)   Xandarians

Who directed 'The Avengers'?

A)   Joss Whedon

B)   Ridley Scott

C)   Spike Jonze

D)   Terry Gilliam

"I don't like bullies. I don't care where they're from." Who said this quote?

A)   Captain America

B)   Dr. Strange

C)   Falcon

D)   Peggy Carter

B) Kree   A) Joss Whedon   A) Captain America

Clint Barton is the name of which character?

A)   Black Panther

B)   Hawkeye

C)   Quicksilver

D)   Vision

Who gifts Loki an all-powerful scepter?

A)   Happy Hogan

B)   Odin

C)   Ronan The Accuser

D)   Thanos

Chris Evens portrays the character Captain America. In what year was the actor born?

A)   1977

B)   1981

C)   1985

D)   1989

B) Hawkeye   D) Thanos   B) 1981

"I recognize the council has made a decision, but given that it's a stupid-ass decision, I've elected to ignore it." Who said this quote?

A)   Ant-Man

B)   Nick Fury

C)   Peter Parker

D)   Tony Stark

What is Captain America's shield made out of?

A)   Adamantium

B)   Lapis Lazuli

C)   Mithril

D)   Vibranium

What is the second film of the MCU?

A)   Captain America: The First Avenger

B)   Iron Man

C)   The Incredible Hulk

D)   Thor

B) Nick Fury   D) Vibranium   C) The Incredible Hulk

Which of the following is NOT an Infinity Stone?

A)   Dream Stone

B)   Mind Stone

C)   Space Stone

D)   Time Stone

Paul Bettany voices J.A.V.I.S. (Iron Man's A.I. assistant). What other character in the MCU does he portray?

A)   Agent Coulson

B)   Red Skull

C)   Vision

D)   Yondu

What is the name of the actor who plays Black Panther in the MCU?

A)   Chadwick Boseman

B)   Daniel Kaluuya

C)   Michael B. Jordan

D)   Winston Duke

A) Dream Stone   C) Vision   A) Chadwick Boseman

What MCU film is the only film not to have an appearance from Samuel
L. Jackson as Nick Fury?

A)   Avengers: Infinity War

B)   Black Panther

C)   The Incredible Hulk

D)   Thor: Ragnarok

In what year was Iron Man 3 released?

A)   2007

B)   2009

C)   2011

D)   2013

Which MCU film is the longest in the franchise at over 181 minutes
long?

A)   Avengers: Age Of Ultron

B)   Avengers: Endgame

C)   Avengers: Infinity War

D)   The Avengers

C) The Incredible Hulk   D) 2013   B) Avengers: Endgame

What is Red Skull's real name?

A)   James Smith

B)   Jaren Sheik

C)   Jorah Smits

D)   Johan Schmidt

Dave Bautista played which MCU character?

A)   Bucky Barnes

B)   Drax

C)   Malekith

D)   Red Skull

Iron Man was the first ever MCU film. In what year was it released?

A)   2002

B)   2004

C)   2006

D)   2008

D) Johan Schmidt   B) Drax   D) 2008

Although Jane Foster is a nurse in the comics, what is her profession in the MCU?

A)   Archaeologist

B)   Astrologist

C)   Chemist

D)   Physicist

Who played the Hulk in the MCU prior to Mark Ruffalo?

A)   Edward Norton

B)   Eric Bana

C)   Matthew Lewis

D)   Ryan Reynolds

How long was Captain America in ice for before being reawakened?

A)   30 years

B)   70 years

C)   110 years

D)   150 years

To which song does baby Groot dance to at the end of 'Guardians of the Galaxy'?

A)   Elton John – I'm Still Standing

B)   Jackson 5 – I Want You Back

C)   Stevie Wonder – Superstition

D)   The Bee Gee's – Stayin' Alive

Who is Loki's biological father?

A)   Laufey

B)   Odin

C)   Surtur

D)   Thanos

The Tesseract is in fact which Infinity Stone?

A)   The Mind Stone

B)   The Reality Stone

C)   The Soul Stone

D)   The Space Stone

B) Jackson 5 – I Want You Back   A) Laufey   D) The Space Stone

How many Infinity Stones exist in the MCU?

A)   6

B)   13

C)   20

D)   1000's

Star-Lord named his ship after which 1980's television star?

A)   Alyssa Milano

B)   Heather Graham

C)   Michelle Pfeiffer

D)   Uma Thurman

What was Sam Wilson prior to becoming Falcon?

A)   Airforce Pilot

B)   Pararescue

C)   Navy Seal

D)   S.W.A.T

A) 6   A) Alyssa Milano   B) Pararescue

What food does Tony Stark suggest the Avengers eat at the end of 'The Avengers'?

A)   Chinese

B)   Ice-Cream

C)   Shawarma

D)   Tacos

Which of the following is Fandral's signature weapon?

A)   Claymore

B)   Flail

C)   Rapier

D)   Scimitar

Anna Boden and who directed the Captain Marvel movie?

A)   Ang Lee

B)   Jon Favreau

C)   Ryan Fleck

D)   Shane Black

C) Shawarma   C) Rapier   C) Ryan Fleck

What is the name of Star-Lords mother?

A)   Anita Quill

B)   Harley Quill

C)   Meredith Quill

D)   Sanza Quill

What super power did Aldrich Killian acquire after being exposed to the Extremis serum?

A)   Flight

B)   Invisibility

C)   Regeneration

D)   Telekinesis

Robert Downey Jr. portrays the character Iron Man. In what year was the actor born?

A)   1955

B)   1960

C)   1965

D)   1970

C) Meredith Quill   C) Regeneration   C) 1965

Who invented the Super Soldier Serum?

A)   Abraham Erskine

B)   Arnim Zola

C)   Darren Cross

D)   Edwin Jarvis

Josh Brolin voices which character in the MCU?

A)   Ancient One

B)   Heimdall

C)   Thanos

D)   The Collector

Benedict Cumberbatch plays the character of Dr. Strange in the MCU. In what country was the actor born?

A)   Canada

B)   England

C)   France

D)   Wales

A) Abraham Erskine   C) Thanos   B) England

What power source fuels Iron Man's suit?

A)   Arc Reactor

B)   Flux Capacitor

C)   Power Stone

D)   Tesseract

Which film came first of the following?

A)   Ant-Man

B)   Avengers: Age of Ultron

C)   Doctor Strange

D)   Guardians Of The Galaxy

Trevor Slattery is an MCU character played by what actor?

A)   Ben Kingsley

B)   Kenneth Choi

C)   Lee Pace

D)   Michael B. Jordan

A) Arc Reactor   D) Guardians of the Galaxy   A) Ben Kingsley

Which is the lowest grossing MCU film to date?

A)   Captain America: The Winter Soldier

B)   Iron Man 2

C)   The Incredible Hulk

D)   Thor: The Dark World

Who voices the character Rocket in the Guardians of the Galaxy films?

A)   Andy Samberg

B)   Bradley Cooper

C)   Mark Hamill

D)   Nathan Fillion

Who founded Marvel Comics back in 1939?

A)   Malcom Wheeler-Nicholson

B)   Martin Goodman

C)   Stan Lee

D)   Walt Disney

C) The Incredible Hulk   B) Bradley Cooper   B) Martin Goodman

In which MCU film does Steve Rogers say; "Trust is what makes an army, not a bunch of guys running around shooting guns."

A)   Captain America: Civil War

B)   Captain America: Winter Soldier

C)   The Avengers: Age of Ultron

D)   The Avengers: Endgame

What is Black Panthers name?

A)   N'Jadaka

B)   N'Jobu

C)   T'Challa

D)   W'Kaba

Who played The Human Torch in the 2015 version of The Fantastic Four?

A)   Jamie Bell

B)   Miles Teller

C)   Michael B. Jordan

D)   Toby Kebbell

B) Captain America: Winter Soldier   C) T'Challa   C) Michael B. Jordan

"Ain't no thing like me, except me!" Who said this quote?

A)   Bruce Banner

B)   Quicksilver

C)   Rocket Raccoon

D)   Yondu

Behind Stan Lee, which actor has appeared most in the MCU?

A)   Chris Evans

B)   Jeremy Renner

C)   Robert Downey Jr.

D)   Samuel L. Jackson

Which of the following characters was NOT turned to dust during Infinity War?

A)   Groot

B)   Mantis

C)   Steve Rogers

D)   T'Challa

C) Rocket Raccoon   D) Samuel L. Jackson   C) Steve Rogers

Tom Holland plays Spider-Man in the MCU. In what year was the actor born?

A)   1994

B)   1996

C)   1998

D)   2000

Who trained Daredevil?

A)   Baron Zemo

B)   Drax the Destroyer

C)   Mandarin

D)   Stick

In which MCU film does Tony Stark say; "I already told you, I don't wanna join your super-secret boy band."

A)   Captain America: Civil War

B)   Iron Man 2

C)   Iron Man 3

D)   The Avengers

B) 1996   D) Stick   B) Iron Man 2

In which MCU film did Thanos first appear?

A)   Captain America: The Winter Soldier

B)   Guardians of the Galaxy 2

C)   Iron Man 3

D)   The Avengers

"DO NOT EVER called me a thesaurus." Who said this quote?

A)   Drax the Destroyer

B)   Maria Hill

C)   Star-Lord

D)   Thor

What is the name of the space dog The Collector keeps in Guardians of the Galaxy?

A)   Buddy

B)   Cosmo

C)   Rocket

D)   Shooter

D) The Avengers   A) Drax the Destroyer   B) Cosmo

What is the name of Thor's sister?

A)	Hela

B)	Shuri

C)	Sif

D)	Valkyrie

What is Deadpools' real name?

A)	William Wylie

B)	Wylie Watson

C)	Wilson Whedon

D)	Winston Wilson

"I ask for one thing in return… a front seat to watch Earth burn." Who said this quote?

A)	Erik Selvig

B)	Loki

C)	Warmachine

D)	Yondu

A) Hela   D) Winston Wilson   B) Loki

What is the S.H.I.E.L.D headquarters called?

A)   Alfheim

B)   Jotunheim

C)   Triskelion

D)   Xandar

What is Luke Cage's real name?

A)   Carl Lucas

B)   James Lyle

C)   Nathan Jones

D)   Rowan Carson

Who rips Ulsses Klaue's arm off?

A)   Abomination

B)   Hulk

C)   Thanos

D)   Ultron

C) Triskelion   A) Carl Lucas   D) Ultron

In what year was the first Deadpool movie released?

A)   2012

B)   2014

C)   2016

D)   2018

What country is Black Panther from?

A)   Asgard

B)   Muspelheim

C)   Svartalfheim

D)   Wakanda

In which MCU film does Peter Parker say; "I'm not collecting tiny spoons. He's collecting tiny spoons."

A)   Iron Man 3

B)   Spider-Man: Far From Home

C)   Spider-Man: Homecoming

D)   The Avengers: Infinity War

C) 2016   D) Wakanda   B) Spider-Man: Far From Home

Samual L. Jackson plays Nick Fury in the MCU. In what U.S city was the actor born?

A)   Houston

B)   Oakland

C)   Philadelphia

D)   Washington DC

What character does Gwyneth Paltrow play in the MCU?

A)   Morgan Stark

B)   Peggy Carter

C)   Pepper Potts

D)   Sharon Carter

What is Storm's real name?

A)   Jean Grey

B)   Kitty Pryde

C)   Madelyne Pryor

D)   Ororo Munroe

D) Washington DC   C) Pepper Potts   D) Ororo Munroe

What is the name of Tony Stark's father?

A)   Howard

B)   Keith

C)   Phillip

D)   Walter

Which of the following is NOT included in the MCU?

A)   Black Panther

B)   Fantastic Four

C)   The Incredible Hulk

D)   Thor: The Dark World

What is Captain Marvel's real name?

A)   Carol Danvers

B)   Darcy Lewis

C)   Jane Foster

D)   Zara Castle

A) Howard   B) Fantastic Four   A) Carol Danvers

What is the name of the actor who plays the villain Kaecilius in the Doctor Strange movie?

A)   Benedict Wong

B)   Chiwetel Ejiofor

C)   Mads Mikkelsen

D)   Scott Adkins

What color is Yondu in the MCU?

A)   Blue

B)   Orange

C)   Purple

D)   Red

"If it comes to saving you, or the kid, or the Time Stone, I will not hesitate to let either of you die." Who says this quote?

A)   Bucky Barnes

B)   Red Skull

C)   Stephen Strange

D)   Tony Stark

C) Mads Mikkelsen   A) Blue   C) Stephen Strange

Chris Pratt plays Star-Lord in the MCU. How tall is the actor?

A)   5'8"

B)   5'11"

C)   6'2"

D)   6'5"

Actor Andy Serkis plays Klaw in the MCU. Klaw appears in two MCU films. Avengers: Age of Ultron and what other movie?

A)   Black Panther

B)   Iron Man 2

C)   The Avengers: Endgame

D)   Thor

"He may have been your father, boy, but he wasn't your daddy?" Who says this quote?

A)   Odin

B)   Thor

C)   Vision

D)   Yondu

C) 6'2"   A) Black Panther   D) Yondu

Yon-Rogg, played by Jude Law, appears in which MCU film?

A)   Black Panther

B)   Captain Marvel

C)   Iron Man 3

D)   Thor: Ragnarok

Which is the first MCU film in which we see Jane Foster?

A)   Spider-Man: Far From Home

B)   Spider-Man: Homecoming

C)   Thor

D)   Thor: The Dark World

Who plays Ant-Man in the MCU?

A)   Aaron Hamill

B)   Michael Rooker

C)   Paul Rudd

D)   Ron Glass

B) Captain Marvel   C) Thor   C) Paul Rudd

Which character does Idris Elba play in the MCU?

A)   Heimdall

B)   Ronan the Accusor

C)   W'Kabi

D)   Zuri

Brie Larson plays Captain Marvel in the MCU. In what country was the actor born?

A)   America

B)   France

C)   Ireland

D)   Poland

"I could choke the life out of you right now, an never turn a shade."

Bruce Banner says this quote in which movie?

A)   Captain America: Civil War

B)   The Avengers

C)   The Avengers: Age of Ultron

D)   The Incredible Hulk

A) Heimdall   A) America   C) The Avengers: Age of Ultron

Which of these actors has NEVER appeared in the MCU?

A)   Donald Gleeson

B)   Jon Favreau

C)   Michael Keaton

D)   Peter Dinklage

How many 'Thor' titles are there in the MCU so far?

A)   2

B)   3

C)   4

D)   5

"No amount of money ever bought a second of time." Who said this quote?

A)   Darcy Lewis

B)   Nebula

C)   Phil Coulson

D)   Tony Stark

How many films in the MCU has Chris Hemsworth's Thor appeared in so far?

A)   6

B)   7

C)   8

D)   9

Tony Stark – "Part of the journey, is the end." In which Marvel film does he say this?

A)   Avengers: Endgame

B)   Captain America: Civil War

C)   Iron Man

D)   Spider-Man: Homecoming

Master of Marvel

The characters, the worlds, the actors and the films

Congratulations! You're now a master of the Marvel universe. You've learned 101 fascinating new facts about the creators of Marvel, how the characters were born and about the behind-the-scenes of the MCU. Then, you were put to the test, and asked 101 tough questions about the world of Marvel. Its actors, the many movies, spanning across unknown worlds and foreign places. How did you go? Did you stump your friends with some difficult questions? Did you learn some things you didn't know before? Either way, now you're a true Marvel fan, and any time anybody asks you an MCU question, you'll surely be able to answer it, and even throw in a fascinating fact to blow people's minds! Now, for one final trivia question, the hardest of them all to answer…

Who is your favourite Marvel character of all time?

Made in the USA
Middletown, DE
28 March 2020